STEP-BY-STEP

PAPIER MÂCHÉ

DERI ROBINS

ILLUSTRATED BY JIM ROBINS

Kingfisher Books

NEW YORK

KINGFISHER

Larousse Kingfisher Chambers Inc.
95 Madison Avenue
New York, New York 10016

First American edition 1993

10 9 8 7 6 5 4 3 2 1 (lib. bdg.)
10 9 8 7 6 5 4 3 2   (pbk.)

Library of Congress Cataloging-
in-Publication Data
Robins, Deri.
    Papier-mâché / Deri Robins.
— 1st American ed.
    p.   cm. — (Step-by-step)
    Summary: Includes an
introduction to making papier-
mâché and instructions for
creating such items as bowls,
masks, animals, and decorations
for special days.
    1. Papier-mâché — Juvenile
literature. [1. Papier-mâché.
2. Handicraft.]   I. Title.
II. Series: Step-by-step
(Kingfisher Books)
TT871.R63   1993
745.54'2 — dc20
92-41102 CIP AC

ISBN 1-85697-927-X (lib. bdg.)
ISBN 1-85697-926-1 (pbk.)

Designed by Ben White
Illustrated by Jim Robins
Photographed by Rolf Cornell,
 SCL Photographic Services
Cover design by Terry Woodley

Printed in Hong Kong

CONTENTS

WHAT YOU NEED

Shown below are the main things you will need to make the models in this book. Before you start on a project, read through the step-by-step instructions to make sure that you have any extra items that are not listed here.

Paper

Although you can use many different types of paper to make papier-mâché (including tissue paper and any paper that is thin and absorbent), newspaper is by far the easiest (and the cheapest) to use.

Glue and Tape

White glue is useful for sticking the papier-mâché parts together. (It can also be used instead of varnish for a final coat.) Use masking tape to hold the parts in place until the glue dries.

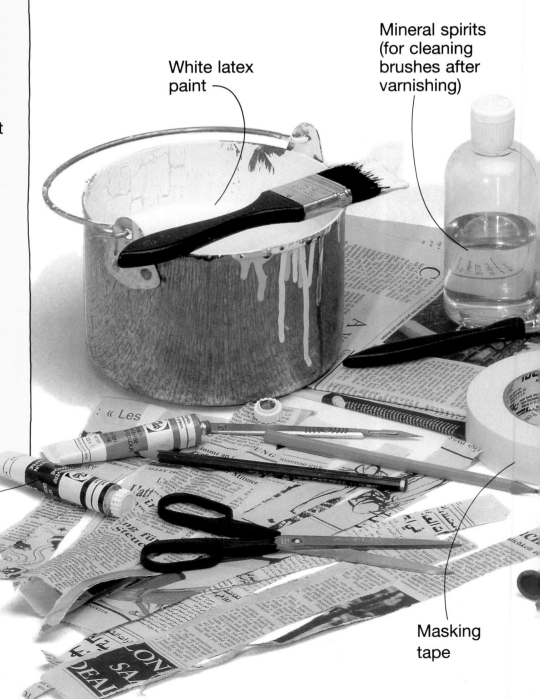

White latex paint

Mineral spirits (for cleaning brushes after varnishing)

Gouache paint

Masking tape

Wallpaper Paste

Most wallpaper pastes contain fungicide — this is poisonous, so keep it away from small children, and don't get it in your eyes, nose, or mouth! You can also make a homemade paste out of flour and water. Heat 6 cups of water and 3 cups of flour in a pan. Keep stirring, until it looks like thick cream. Leave to cool.

SAFETY TIP:
You will need to use a sharp knife to make some of the things in this book. Be sure that you always ask an adult to help you.

Junk

Keep a collection of junk, such as cardboard tubes, cereal boxes, bottles, string, wire, foil, and corrugated paper. For some of the models, you will also need some modeling clay, and a bag of balloons.

Paints and Varnish

You will need white latex, gouache, or poster paints, and some varnish (see page 8). You will also need a small brush for decorating, a medium-sized paintbrush, and a thin brush for fine details.

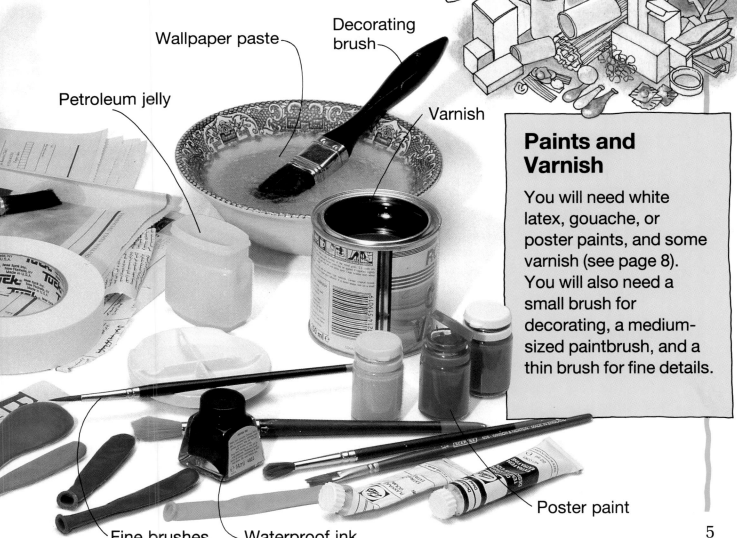

Wallpaper paste

Decorating brush

Petroleum jelly

Varnish

Fine brushes

Waterproof ink

Poster paint

5

BASIC TECHNIQUES

Most of the models in the book are made by pasting strips of paper over a *mold* (such as a bowl), or a *framework* (such as a cardboard box). You can also make pulp, which is modeled just like clay.

Using Molds

Always grease your molds with lots of petroleum jelly before you put on the papier-mâché. This makes it much easier to remove the mold later on.

Using Frameworks

Bottles, tubes, boxes, and other pieces of junk can be used as frameworks for papier-mâché. Unlike molds, these are not removed when the paper is dry.

Paper Strips

Always tear the paper rather than cutting it — this gives a smoother finish. It's a good idea to work with two piles of different-colored paper, and to change color when you start a new layer — this helps you to see where one layer ends and the new one starts.

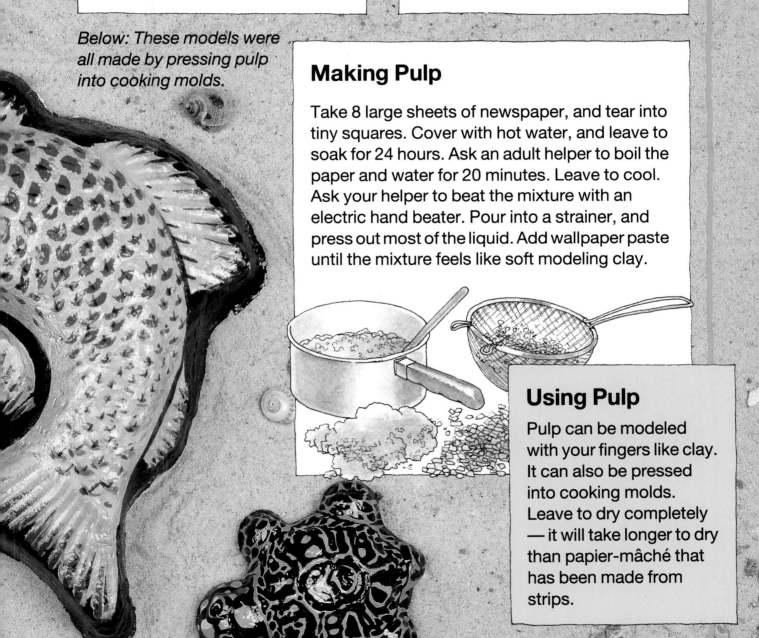

Pasting Strips

Make the paste, following the directions on the package. Cover each strip with paste, and smooth over the mold or framework. Overlap them slightly, until the object is completely covered. Repeat for all other layers.

Drying Out

When you've put on all the layers, leave the papier-mâché to dry out completely in a warm, dry place. As a rough guide, a bowl made from 7 layers of papier-mâché will take two to three days to dry out.

Below: These models were all made by pressing pulp into cooking molds.

Making Pulp

Take 8 large sheets of newspaper, and tear into tiny squares. Cover with hot water, and leave to soak for 24 hours. Ask an adult helper to boil the paper and water for 20 minutes. Leave to cool. Ask your helper to beat the mixture with an electric hand beater. Pour into a strainer, and press out most of the liquid. Add wallpaper paste until the mixture feels like soft modeling clay.

Using Pulp

Pulp can be modeled with your fingers like clay. It can also be pressed into cooking molds. Leave to dry completely — it will take longer to dry than papier-mâché that has been made from strips.

DECORATING IDEAS

Bright poster or gouache paint brings papier-mâché magically to life! Experiment with color — bold primary colors and soft pastels both work well, while gold and silver can make a model look as if it is made of metal. Always give your papier-mâché a coat of white latex before you begin, and finish with at least one coat of varnish.

If you don't feel confident enough to paint a design onto your models, try some of the decorating ideas shown below.

Spattering

Paint a base color over your papier-mâché. Dip an old toothbrush or a nailbrush in a second color. Flick the brush gently with your finger, so that the paint spatters over the surface.

Rag Rolling

Instead of painting your papier-mâché with a brush, try dipping a crumpled rag or a piece of sponge into light-colored paint and then pressing or rolling it lightly over the surface. Repeat with one or more darker colors for a mottled effect that looks rather like stone (see the Greek urn on page 13). This painting technique is useful for covering up a bumpy surface!

Torn Paper

Bowls and plates can look fantastic if you use torn-up colored tissue paper or wrapping paper as a final layer. Scraps of silk can even be glued on in this way. You could also try painting on a base coat in the usual way and decorating with a mosaic made up of tiny squares of paper (see page 11).

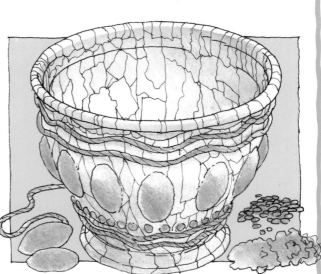

Découpage

Paint a base color onto your papier-mâché. Cut out pictures or shapes from magazines, wrapping paper, or plain colored paper, and glue them to the painted surface.

Raised Surfaces

Glue pieces of string, split peas, shapes cut from cardboard, or lumps of pulp onto papier-mâché before painting with white latex.

9

BOWLS AND PLATES

Lots of objects can be used as molds for bowls, plates, and trays. In addition to dishes from the kitchen, you could use a ball or a blown-up balloon. Use at least seven layers of paper — more if you want your bowl or plate to be really thick and strong.

1 Cover the inside of a bowl, wok, or plate with petroleum jelly. Do the same around the rim and the outside edge.

2 Paste on at least 7 layers of paper strips. Leave in a warm place for 2-3 days, or until completely dry.

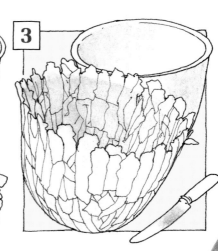

3 Run a blunt knife between the papier-mâché and the mold and gently ease the papier-mâché off.

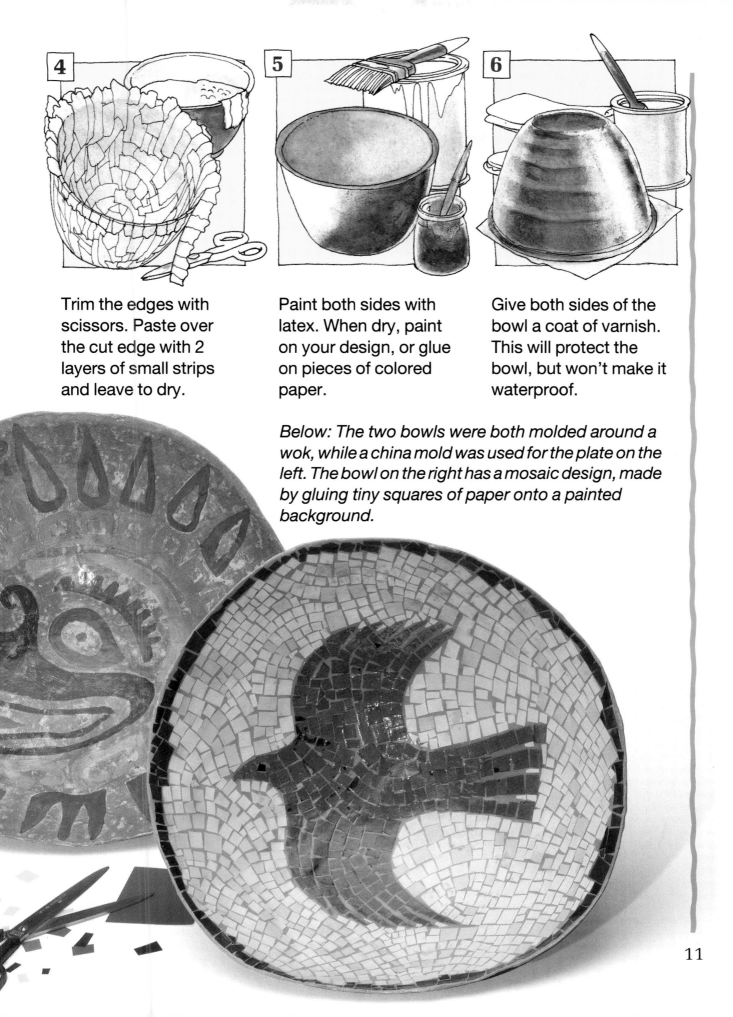

4 Trim the edges with scissors. Paste over the cut edge with 2 layers of small strips and leave to dry.

5 Paint both sides with latex. When dry, paint on your design, or glue on pieces of colored paper.

6 Give both sides of the bowl a coat of varnish. This will protect the bowl, but won't make it waterproof.

Below: The two bowls were both molded around a wok, while a china mold was used for the plate on the left. The bowl on the right has a mosaic design, made by gluing tiny squares of paper onto a painted background.

Legs and Bases

Glue an empty tape roll under the bowl. If you want, you can glue a circle of cardboard under it. Or make feet from small cones (page 14). Cover with 2 layers of strips.

Making Rims

Coat small strips of paper with paste, and roll up into a thin sausage shape. Wrap it around the outside of the rim, and hold it in place with extra paper strips.

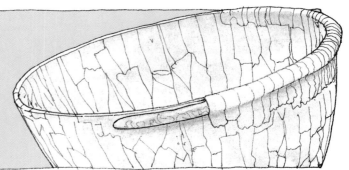

Making Handles

Cut handles from cardboard. Bend back the flaps, and glue to the sides of the bowl. Or make slits with a knife, and glue in the ends of the handles. Paper over with strips.

Rolled-up Roses

Make roses by tearing strips of paper, about 4 x 10 inches. Cover one side with paste, and fold in half. Paste again, and roll around the end of a paintbrush to make a rose. Paste onto the side of the bowl, with leaves cut from cardboard. Paper over the leaves and the seams with 2 layers of strips.

The "Greek urn" was rag-rolled (see page 8) and decorated with pictures cut out of a magazine. The yellow bowl has cardboard cone legs. The third bowl was decorated with string, painted blue, and then rubbed over with a rag dipped in gold paint.

PIGGY BANK

Balloons are often used as molds for papier-mâché. Here's a piggy bank to make — just add a yogurt container for a snout, pieces of cardboard for ears and legs, and a pipe cleaner for a tail. To collect your savings, just cut a hole in the bottom — you could use a plastic cap to plug the hole.

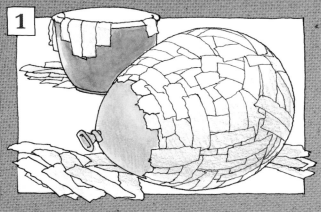

1

Blow up a round or an oval balloon, and cover with petroleum jelly. Paste on 5 layers of paper strips, and leave to dry for about 2 days.

2

Cut 2 ears from cardboard. Draw around a small bowl onto cardboard to make 2 circles, and cut out. Cut circles in half, and tape into cones for legs.

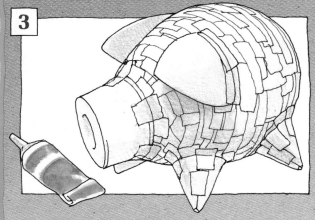

3

Burst the balloon with a pin, and pull it out. Paste the ears, legs, and the yogurt container onto the body with white glue. Hold in place with masking tape.

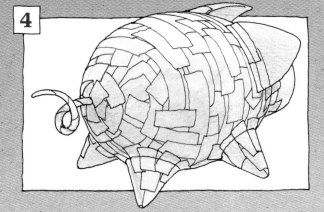

4

Make a hole at the back with a pin. Bend a pipe cleaner into a curly tail, push into the hole, and glue in place. Cover with two layers of strips.

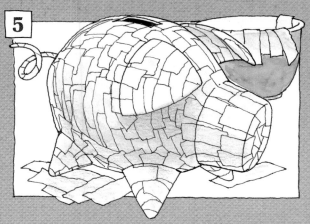

5

Cover the ears, legs, and snout with 2 layers of paper. Leave to dry. Ask an adult to cut a slit in the top with a sharp knife.

Pigs don't have to be pink! Why not decorate with stars, flowers, polka dots, or the owner's name?

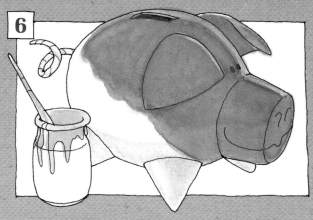

6

Paint your piggy bank with a good strong color. When it's finished, use at least one layer of varnish to protect and strengthen it.

MAKING MASKS

All kinds of wonderful masks can be made from papier-mâché. Try gluing on string, yarn, or tinfoil — our tiger has ears and a nose made out of cardboard and whiskers made from bristles taken from an old brush. A gold glitter pen was used to add shimmering highlights to the stripes.

1

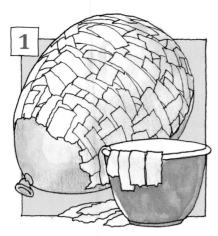

Blow up a balloon to your head size. Cover half with petroleum jelly, and paste on 5 layers of paper.

2

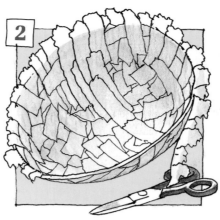

Dry for 2 days. Take the mask off, and trim with scissors. Ask an adult to cut out the eyes with a sharp knife.

3

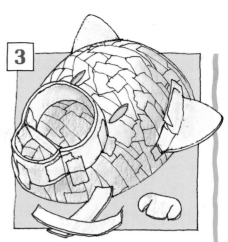

Make the ears and nose from cardboard, and glue them to the head. Tape in place until the glue dries.

4

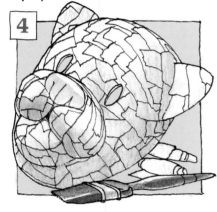

Paste 2 layers of paper over the ears and across the nose. Pad the sides with rolls of pasted paper.

5

When dry, paint both sides with latex. Color with poster paint, and finish with two coats of clear varnish.

6

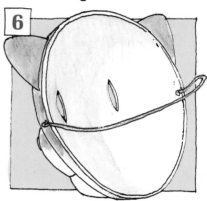

Use a thick needle to make a hole on each side. Thread with elastic, and adjust to fit the size of your head.

Try making scary masks for Halloween, crazy carnival masks, or funny faces for plays and disguises.

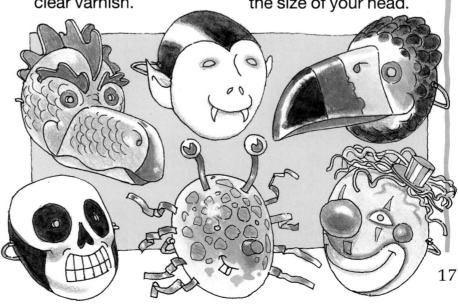

FLYING MACHINES

Make hot-air balloons and airships from different-shaped balloons. Paint bright designs on them, add a coat of glossy varnish, and hang from the ceiling with thread.

1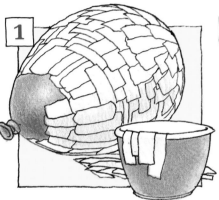

Blow up an oval balloon, and grease with petroleum jelly. Cover with 6 layers of paper strips, and dry.

2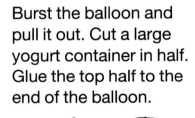

Burst the balloon and pull it out. Cut a large yogurt container in half. Glue the top half to the end of the balloon.

3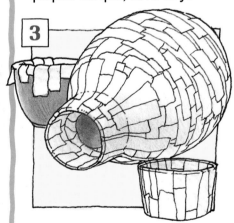

Cover both container halves with 3 layers of strips, papering over the joint between the balloon and container.

4

Seal the balloon and basket with white latex. Paint brightly and finish with a coat of varnish.

5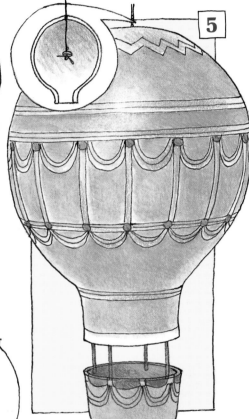

Push a threaded needle down through the balloon, and attach a button. Knot the thread under the button. Pull the button up to the top of the balloon. Attach the basket using a needle and thread.

18

Airship

Cover a long balloon with paper strips. Glue 2 curved pieces of cardboard together and support with a strip of cardboard in the middle. Cut a propellor, and attach with a pin.

Loop lengths of thread through the gondola, and hang them over the airship. Glue a bent paper clip into the airship to hang it up.

19

FUN FRUIT

Fill a bowl with fake fruit — or pile it up on top of a carnival hat, as shown on page 23. Delicious-looking vegetables can also be made in a very similar way — or how about a hamburger and fries?

Bananas and Watermelons

Make a simple framework by taping curved pieces of cardboard together (it doesn't matter if the edges don't meet exactly). Paper over with 3 layers of strips.

Grapes, Cherries, and Strawberries

Make these from little balls of paper pulp. When the grapes are dry, glue them in a bunch onto a piece of cardboard.

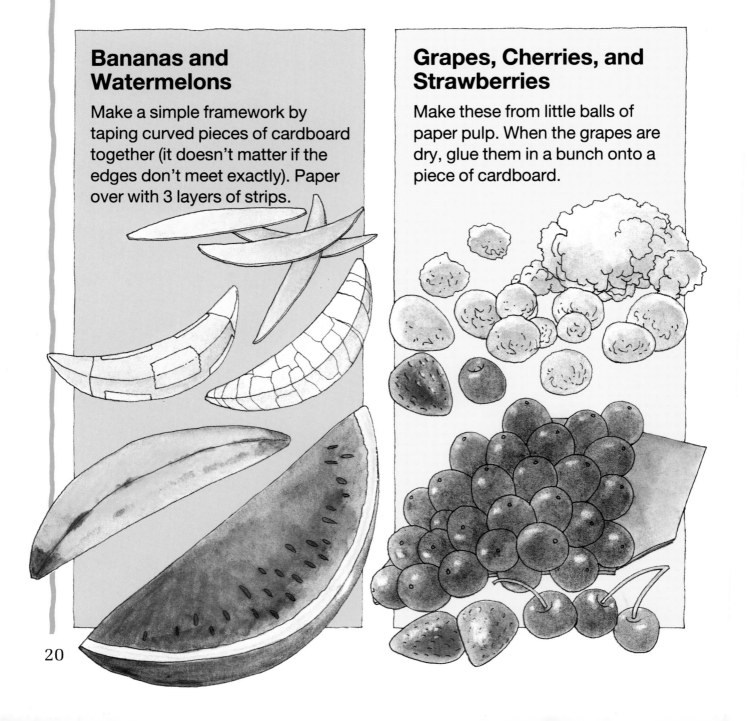

Oranges and Lemons

Crumple up a piece of paper towel. Wrap another piece around the first one, then add a third and fourth. Use masking tape to mold the paper into the shape you need. Cover with 3 layers of pasted strips (it's easiest if you let each layer dry before you add the next). Paint to look as real as possible.

Pineapple

Blow up a small balloon. Cover with 7 layers of strips, and leave to dry. Cut a wide strip of thin cardboard, and cut into pointed leaves with scissors. Glue to the top of the balloon as shown, and paper over the joint. Paint the base color, then the main sections, and finally the detail in each section.

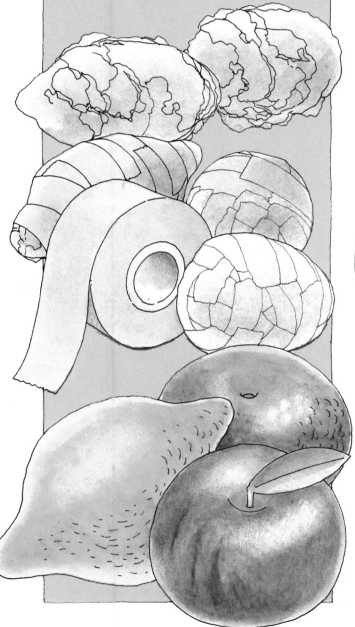

FRUIT HAT

This incredible carnival hat may look top heavy — but as it's made from papier-mâché, it's very light and easy to wear.

First, you will need to blow up a balloon until it's the size of your head. Cover with seven layers of paper strips, and leave until completely dry.

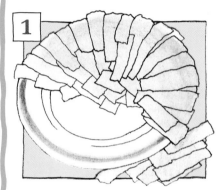

1 Cover both sides of a paper plate with 3 layers of pasted strips. Leave to dry.

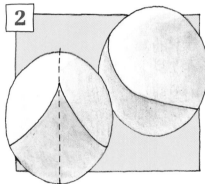

2 Copy the pattern above onto the covered balloon, and cut away the bottom section.

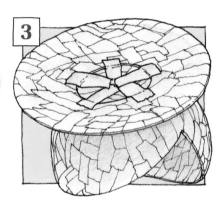

3 Glue and tape the plate to the hat — this is easier if you cut a hole in the base of the plate.

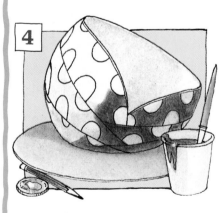

4 Paper over the joint and the cut edges with small paper strips. When dry, paint and varnish the hat in the usual way.

5 Glue papier-mâché fruit, plastic fruit, or flowers onto the plate. Hook real or papier-mâché earrings (see page 36) onto the hat.

6

HELMET

Silver poster paint and a coat of matte varnish are used to make this helmet look as if it is made of metal.

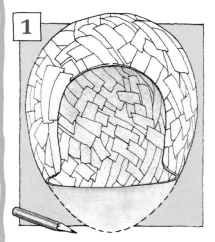

1 Cover a balloon with 7 layers of strips. When dry, copy the pattern shown here, and cut out with scissors.

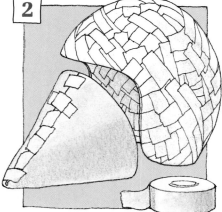

2 Make a cone from a large semicircle of cardboard. The cone should fit snugly over the front of the helmet.

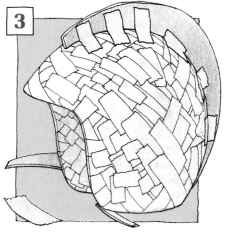

3 Cut a crest out of cardboard, and tape to the top. Don't worry if there are gaps between the crest and the helmet.

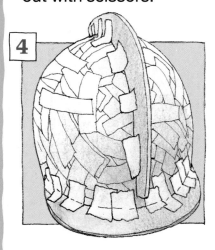

4 Cut a smaller cardboard crescent for the back of the helmet, and tape in position.

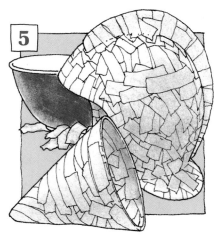

5 Cover the cone, crest, and back of the helmet with 3 layers of papier-mâché. Leave to dry.

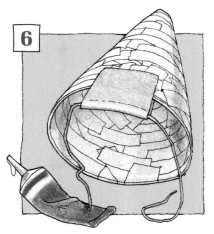

6 Fold a strip of cardboard in half. Lay a piece of string along the crease, and glue to the cone.

24

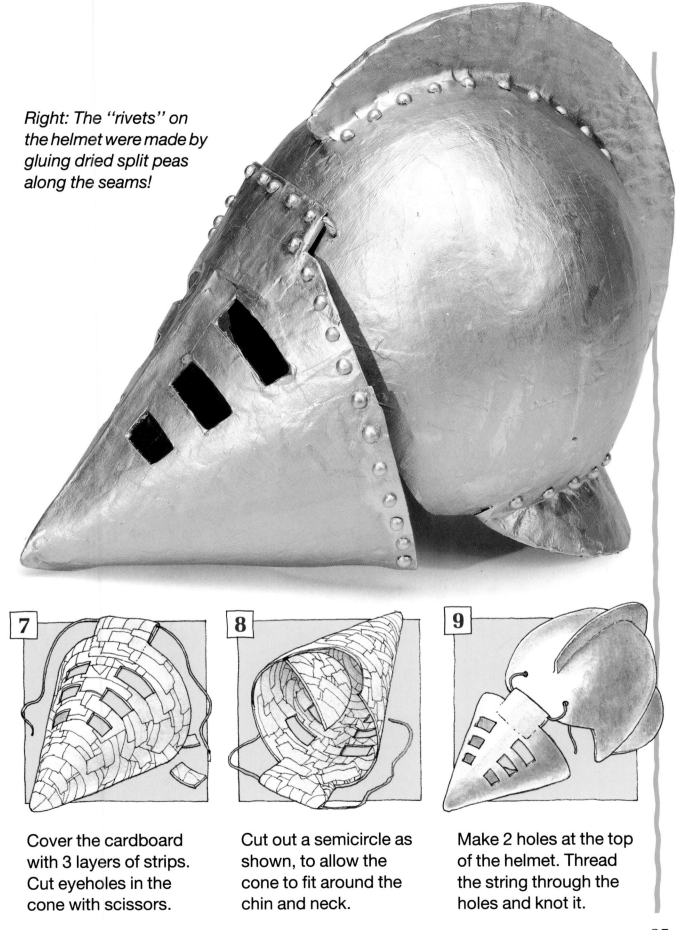

Right: The "rivets" on the helmet were made by gluing dried split peas along the seams!

7 Cover the cardboard with 3 layers of strips. Cut eyeholes in the cone with scissors.

8 Cut out a semicircle as shown, to allow the cone to fit around the chin and neck.

9 Make 2 holes at the top of the helmet. Thread the string through the holes and knot it.

MAKE A MOBILE

Papier-mâché shapes can be hung with thread from coat-hangers, or from bars made from dowels or balsa wood. Hang the mobile up near a door or window, where currents of air will make the shapes spin around.

1

Fold a piece of cardboard in half. Draw or trace 5 mobile shapes onto the cardboard, and cut out with scissors.

2

Staple the tops and sides, and stuff with tissue paper. Staple the gaps, and cover with 3 layers of pasted strips.

3

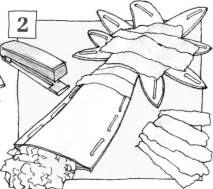

Paint and varnish in the usual way. When dry, thread the top of each shape using a needle.

4

Cut one length of balsa wood of 18 inches and two of 8 inches. Sandpaper until smooth, then paint and varnish. Make holes at each end with a needle.

5

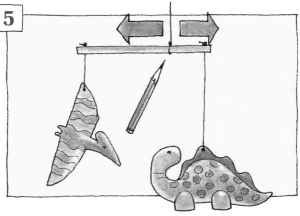

Thread two mobiles onto each of the short bars, as shown. Tie a piece of thread to the middle of the bar, and move it up and down until it balances.

6 Push a threaded needle through this "balancing point." Attach the two short bars to the long bar, and add the fifth shape. Hang up from the top bar, finding the balancing point as before.

PIRATE PUPPET

Here's a simple puppet that doesn't need wires or strings — just hold the body under the cloth and wiggle it around! First, blow up a round balloon and cover with six layers of paper.

Once you have mastered this basic shape, you can go on to design a whole theaterful of puppet characters!

1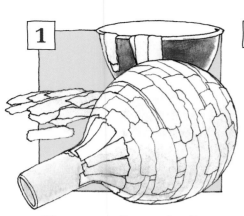

Glue a cardboard roll to the neck. Cover with 3 layers of pasted strips.

2

Cut cardboard features. Glue to the face, and cover with 3 layers.

3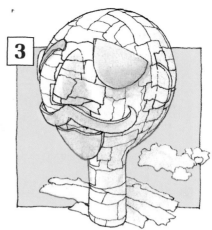

Mold ears and nose from pasted paper strips. Leave to dry.

4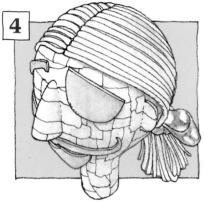

Glue string to the puppet's head. When dry, tie a knot in the back with more string.

5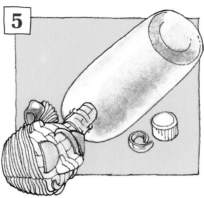

Cut the top off a plastic bottle, and push in the puppet's head. Glue to hold it.

6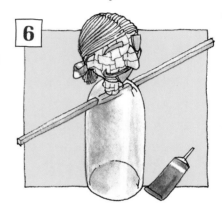

Cut a cross in each side. Push through a piece of balsa wood, and glue in place.

7

Paint the head, and glue on a scrap of material for a headband. Add a gold earring, if you have one.

8

Dress in a child's (or doll's) T-shirt, or sew 2 T-shaped fabric pieces. Tie a bandanna around the neck.

9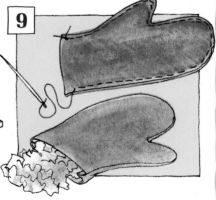

Make two small gloves from scraps, as shown. Stuff with cotton and glue one to each of the wooden arms.

29

SPECIAL DAYS

Lightweight papier-mâché is great for making Christmas tree ornaments. Try using gold and silver paint and glitter pens to add some sparkle. On page 32 you will find some ideas for celebrating Easter and Halloween.

A Christmas Angel

Cut wings out of cardboard. Cover with a thick layer of pulp (see page 7). Lay a sheet of plastic wrap over the pulp, and roll lightly with a rolling pin. Trim the edges with a knife.

Push a paper clip into the back, as shown, and leave to dry out. Mold the head from a ball of pulp. When dry, glue to the wings. Paint and varnish as usual.

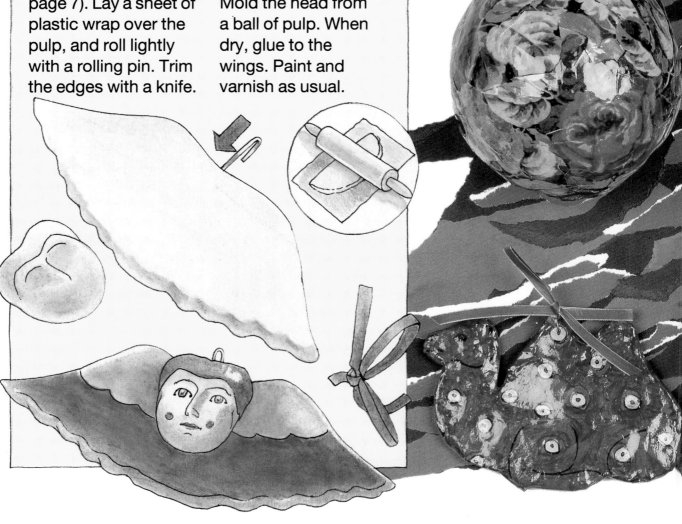

Balls

Blow up a small round balloon, and cover with 6 layers of strips. When dry, burst the balloon, remove, and paper over the hole. Paint and varnish the balls, or glue on scraps of wrapping paper. Push a bent paper clip through the top, and glue in place.

Christmas Shapes

Cut Christmas shapes out of cardboard, and paper both sides with 3 layers of strips. Paint them and varnish as usual. Make a hole through the top and thread with ribbon.

31

Easter Egg

Cover an oval balloon with 7 layers of strips. When dry, ask an adult to cut it in half with a sharp knife. Glue a long strip of cardboard to the inside rim of one of the halves, and cover the rims of both halves with 2 layers of small strips. When dry, both halves should fit together as shown below. Paint and varnish the egg.

Halloween Pumpkin

Cover about $3/4$ of an oval balloon with 7 layers of strips. Leave to dry. Cut the top of the pumpkin into points with scissors, and ask and adult to cut out the eyes, nose, and mouth with a sharp knife. Paint bright orange on the outside, and black inside. Varnish, then thread each side with thick thread and hang up.

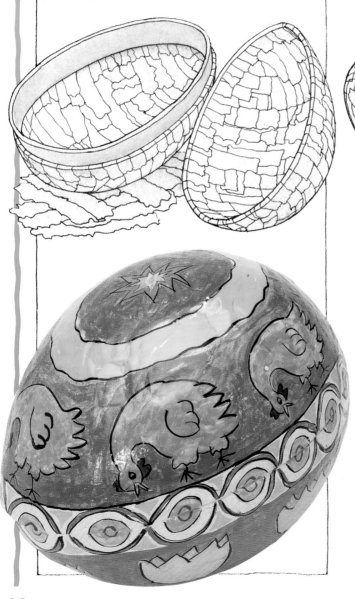

ROSE BOX

Shoe boxes, hatboxes, candy boxes —
all these can be transformed by
papier-mâché!

1. Draw around the box on thick cardboard. Add an extra $3/4$ inch all around, and cut out to make a base. Repeat to make a lid.

2. Cut a piece of cardboard, $1/3$ inch less wide and $1/3$ inch less long than the box. Glue this piece to the middle of the lid.

3. Glue the box to the middle of the base. Cover the box and lid with 3 layers of strips.

4. Add roses and leaves (see page 12) to the box. Paint and varnish.

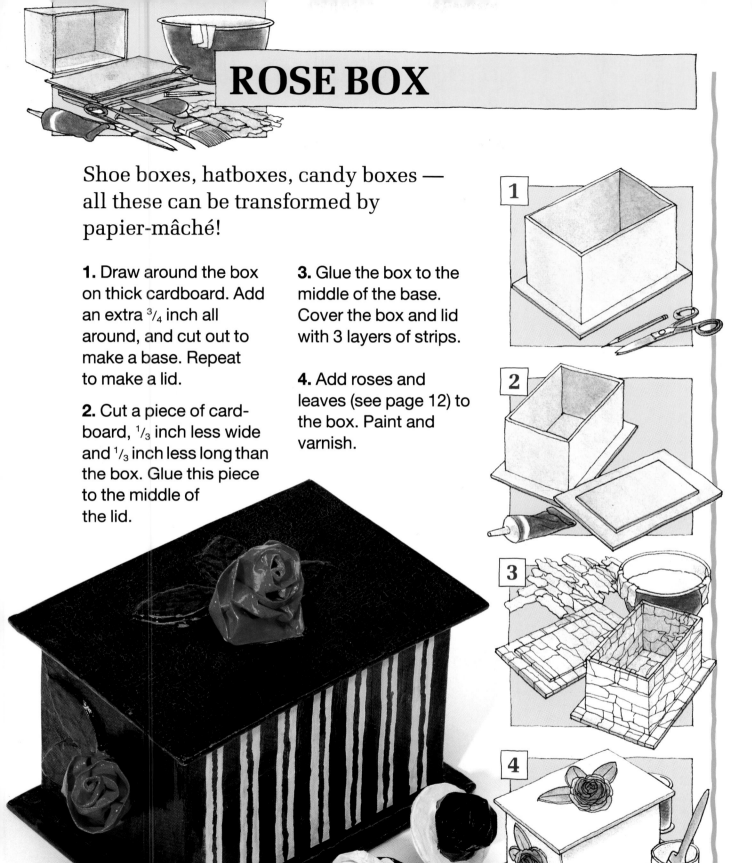

33

UNUSUAL GIFTS

Museums and history books are a good source of ideas for papier-mâché. The shape of this object comes from a picture of an ancient Chinese burial urn!

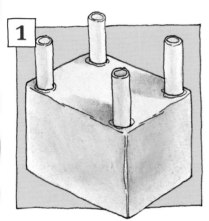

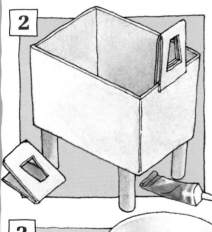

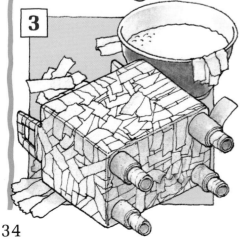

1. Glue legs to a deep box — these are made by gluing thin cardboard rolls to the bottom. You could also make cone legs for the box, as shown on page 14.

2. Glue on handles made from folded cardboard.

3. Cover with 3 layers of strips, adding more around the tops of the legs. Paint and varnish.

Molds come in lots of different shapes and sizes. Use them to make great-looking lids for boxes.

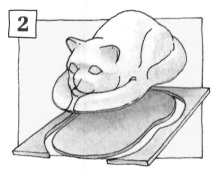

1. Grease the inside of the mold with petroleum jelly. Press in a thick layer of paper pulp, and leave to dry.

2. Ease out of the mold. Draw around the outline on cardboard, cut out and glue to the bottom. Cover with two layers of strips.

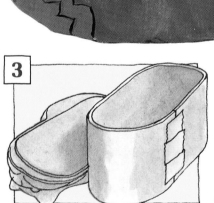

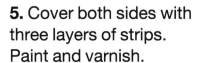

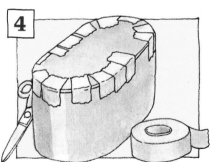

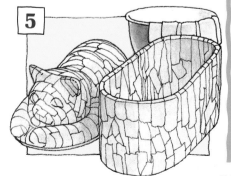

3. Cut a strip of cardboard. Curl it into an oval shape, making it just smaller than the lid. The lid should be able to rest on the top. Tape firmly in place.

4. Cut a bottom for the box out of cardboard, and glue in place.

5. Cover both sides with three layers of strips. Paint and varnish.

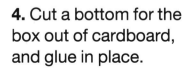

JEWELRY

Because papier-mâché is so light, it can be used to make really large, dramatic pieces of jewelry. The metal attachments (called *findings*) can be bought quite cheaply from craft and hobby stores.

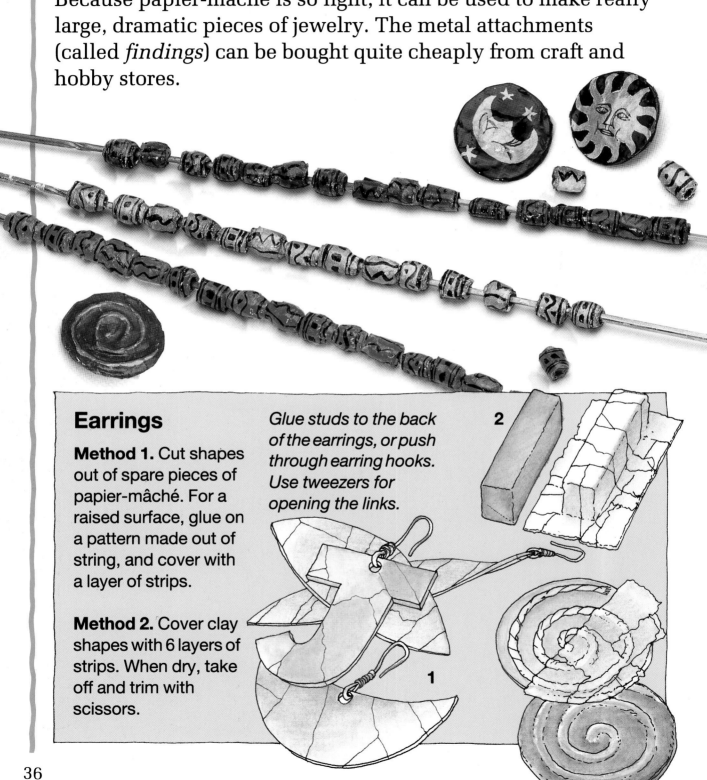

Earrings

Method 1. Cut shapes out of spare pieces of papier-mâché. For a raised surface, glue on a pattern made out of string, and cover with a layer of strips.

Method 2. Cover clay shapes with 6 layers of strips. When dry, take off and trim with scissors.

Glue studs to the back of the earrings, or push through earring hooks. Use tweezers for opening the links.

2

1

Beads

Cut lots of long, V-shaped strips of paper. Cover each strip with paste, and wrap around a knitting needle. Slip off, and leave to dry. Paint, varnish, and thread to make a necklace.

Bracelets

Cover an empty tape roll with 3 layers of strips. Add texture with glued-on dried pasta shells or string. Paint and varnish.

More Baubles

Make huge buttons from papier-mâché, or try decorating combs and barrettes. Use glitter for a sparkly effect — or cover the pieces with scraps of silk or tissue paper.

SPOTTED DOG

This dog's body is made from a large cardboard tube, and the legs are made from smaller tubes. Giraffes, zebras, lions, and tigers (in fact, any kind of animal you like) can all be made in a similar way.

1

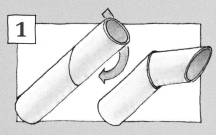

Cut a small tube in half and glue together as shown. Cut the top of the tube diagonally.

2

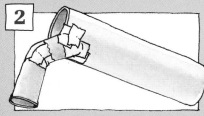

Repeat with a second tube. Tape to one end of the large tube, to make the back legs.

3

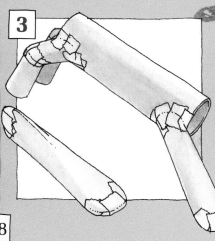

Flatten both ends of two more small tubes. Tape them to the front end of the body.

4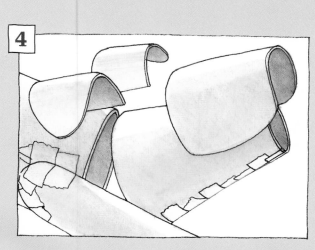

5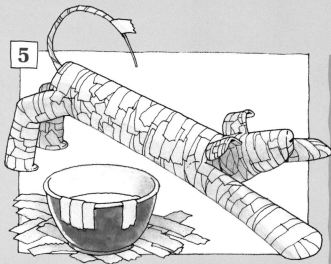

Glue a yogurt container, or a cardboard cone, to the front of the tube. Cut a flap for the muzzle as shown, and glue to the head. Add ears made out of cardboard.

Cut small circles and glue under the back legs to make paws. Cover the dog with 4 layers of papier-mâché. Add extra strips around the joints and around

the big tube to pad out the shape. Push in a tail made out of garden wire, and cover with 3 layers of strips. When dry, paint and varnish in the usual way.

MORE IDEAS

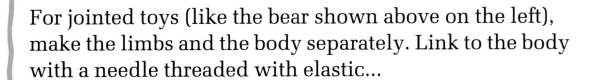

Try making some small toys from papier-mâché — mold the shapes from modeling clay and cover with six layers of tiny paper strips. When dry, cut in half and take off the mold. Glue the halves back together, and paint. Old bath toys, like the duck on the right, also make good molds...

For jointed toys (like the bear shown above on the left), make the limbs and the body separately. Link to the body with a needle threaded with elastic...

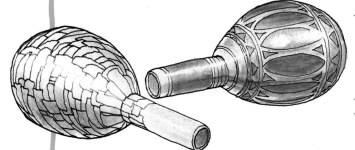

Use balloons and cardboard tubes to make maracas like the ones on the left! Fill with dried peas or beans...

Large cardboard boxes can be turned into fantasy buildings with papier-mâché. By adding "extras" — made with cardboard, you could make a castle, a garage, or even a whole dollhouse. Make furniture from tubes of cardboard, and other scraps.

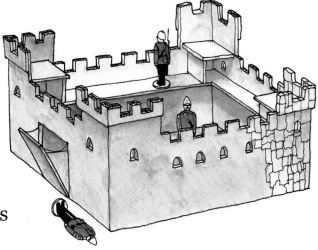